spot and stripe

Five Mile, an imprint of
Bonnier Publishing Australia
Level 6, 534 Church Street,
Richmond, Victoria 3121

This edition published 2016

Printed in China 5 4 3 2 1

spot and Stripe

Anna Shuttlewood

The Five Mile Press

Spot is a leopard.

Stripe is a zebra.

Spot and Stripe are best friends.

Like most best friends, Spot and Stripe
like to spend all their time together.

In the day, they lie under the sun and make
up stories from pictures in the clouds.

At night, they lie under the moon and look for shooting stars.

Spot and Stripe love being best friends.

But there is just one little thing that they
wish they could change.

Spot and Stripe want to look the same as each other.
"I want to be just like you!" says Spot.
"That's funny," says Stripe.
"Because I want to be just like YOU!"

So they decide to spend a day teaching each other all about how to be a leopard and a zebra.

Stripe shows Spot how to pick blackberries without getting prickles on his nose.

Spot shows Stripe how to chase birds without getting
lost in the tall grass.

Stripe shows Spot how to cross the river safely.

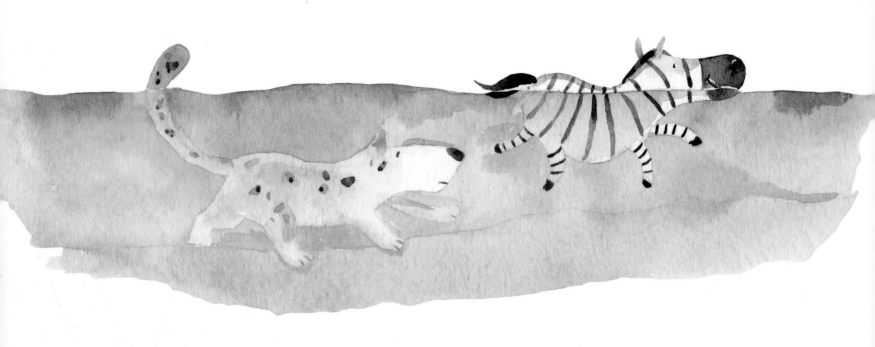

Spot shows Stripe how
to easily climb a tree.

Spot and Stripe are very pleased with their lessons.
Spot thinks he will make an excellent zebra.
Stripe thinks she can be a wonderful leopard.

But then Spot and Stripe catch
a glimpse of their reflections.

They still look like the exact same
Spot and Stripe. And they don't look
anything alike.

Spot and Stripe are very disappointed.
"How can we look so different when we are the same
on the inside?" says Stripe.
"How can we be best friends if we look nothing alike?" says Spot.

So they sit down to think.
    Then they lie down to think.

They really do a lot of thinking.

Suddenly Spot jumps up.
"I have an idea, Stripe!"
Stripe leaps to her feet.
"I have an idea too, Spot!"

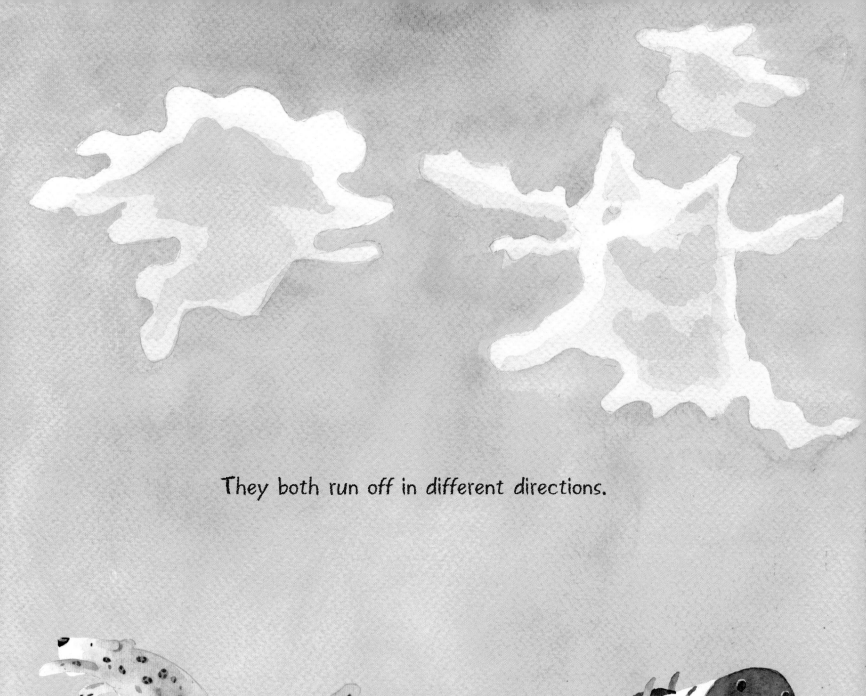

They both run off in different directions.

And when they return, Spot and Stripe almost don't recognise each other. They both look exactly the same — because they are both covered in mud!

Spot and Stripe are so excited!
Finally, they look like real best friends should!

They chase birds.

And gobble down blackberries.

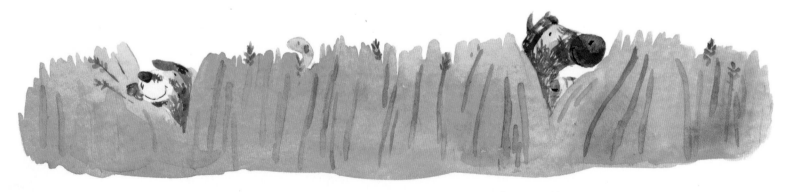

And play hide-and-seek amongst the tall grass.

And eventually, tired from all the excitement,
they sit down to look at cloud pictures.

"Hey, Stripe?" says Spot.

"Everything is so nice. But do you know what?
I missed your stripes while we were chasing birds.
I really like your stripes."

"I missed your spots too!" says Stripe.
"I like the way you really are!"

"And I like the way YOU really are!
I'm so happy when you're stripy!" says Spot.

"Maybe it doesn't matter that we're different
on the outside?" says Stripe.

"Maybe it really doesn't," says Spot.
"No matter if you're spotty or stripy or covered
in mud, you're still my best friend!"

Spot and Stripe are so happy
      that they dance all the way home.

Where they meet two people who are not
so happy — their mums!